Mrs. Portree's Pony

Mrs. Portree's Pony

LYNN HALL

Charles Scribner's Sons
NEW YORK

Copyright © 1986 Lynn Hall

Library of Congress Cataloging-in-Publication Data
Hall, Lynn.   Mrs. Portree's pony.
Summary: Addie, a foster child who feels unloved,
seeks comfort in the company of a beautiful pony and
begins an enriching relationship with his owner, a
proud woman who has alienated and lost her own daughter.
[1. Ponies—Fiction.   2. Foster home care—Fiction.
3. Mothers and daughters—Fiction]   I. Title.
PZ7.H1458Mr   1986   [Fic]   85-43353
ISBN 0-684-18576-8
Published simultaneously in Canada
by Collier Macmillan Canada, Inc.

1 3 5 7 9 11 13 15 17 19   F/C   20 18 16 14 12 10 8 6 4 2

Printed in the United States of America

Mrs. Portree's Pony

1

Addie Harvey did not want to be thirteen. She didn't want to let go of her childhood yet, because her childhood had not yet given her what she needed from it.

As all children do, Addie Harvey needed to feel that she was loved, in that easy, generous way that people love children. Since no one had loved her in her childhood, Addie reasoned, how could she expect to be loved ever in her life? Childhood is when people are most lovable, and even her childhood hadn't been enough to do the trick for Addie. Not yet. And it was over, today. Today she was thirteen and her unsatisfying childhood was over, to be replaced by a part of her life that was bound to be worse.

Following an urge she didn't fully understand, an urge to do a childish thing, to hang onto her youth until she had wrung out of it what she needed, Addie went walking up the creek.

The Everetts' house, where Addie stayed, was at the edge of town, although Amherst was such a tiny town that almost every house could be said to be at its edge. The house was tall but narrow and angular, built of logs, with doors and window shutters painted dark green. Many of the older houses in that part of Wisconsin were built of logs because the pine forests had had to be cleared in order to make room for houses and towns. Some of the old pines still stood, along with the maples and oaks that shaded the village. A semicircle of pines curled around the back edge of the Everetts' lawn, and twisting among their feet ran Addie's creek.

It was a clear, shallow creek about four or five feet wide, less than a foot deep, and running almost level with the land so that a child, or a small thirteen-year-old, could sit on the bank with her feet resting on the sandy creek bottom and rest her elbows on her knees and cup her chin in her palms and watch the water swirl around her ankles.

The water was clear and cool, even now in August. Through it, the sandy creek bed and its gray and blue and violet stones could be seen magnified by the water, bigger and brighter than life.

There was nothing unusual about Addie wading into the creek. The creek had been her friend for all of the seven years she'd lived with the Everetts; sometimes it had seemed her only friend. She'd waded and sat and splashed and rolled in it for seven summers, and taken long running skids on it for six winters, and shared it reluctantly and jealously with Walt Junior and Lori Everett, who were younger than Addie.

But today, for the first time, she walked into the creek with her shoes on and began walking upstream, away from town. It was a childish thing to do and it satisfied her mood. She wanted someone to come along and say, "Hey, you crazy kid, what are you doing getting your shoes wet?"

Then she could make some smart-aleck remark and feel even more satisfyingly miserable. But of course no one could see her way down here at the far end of backyards.

And of course they were only tennis shoes; she wasn't really doing them any harm by getting them wet. They felt funny with the water squishing out of the spongy soles each time she took a step, that was the only thing. And it gave her a peculiar feeling to be wading and not feel the sand and stones against the skin of her feet. Funny, but not bad.

3

"I should have thought of this before," she said out loud.

The creek wound through three more back-yards before it got clear of the town. Then it ran almost straight, through an empty pasture where long, rich grass bent over its banks and trailed in the water. The banks were at Addie's knee level. When she walked close to the edge, the grass stroked her legs and made her shiver.

Creek and highway ran parallel here, separated only by a slice of pasture. A car went by and the people in it turned their heads to look at Addie.

"Child wading in creek on a summer day," Addie said. "Picture of happy childhood. Someone should make a painting of it and call it that. Then maybe it would be true."

Creek and highway curved toward each other then and crossed like fingers crossing, the highway bending south toward Wautoma, the creek ducking under it through a round metal tunnel. It wasn't enough of a creek to need a bridge. Addie bent her head down and walked through the culvert, feeling the ridges of the metal under her soles and wishing a car would roar over her. None did.

She paused and squatted to look at the bright circle of world framed by the far end of the culvert.

It looked more beautiful, more important, framed that way and cut off from its surroundings: the creek twisting away among trees, the split-rail fence around the Allens' yard, a corner of the fenced dog run where the Allens' hunting dogs lived, and in the distance a range of rocky hills.

A dog would have been nice, Addie thought. She'd had no real hopes for a dog for her birthday. Walt Junior was allergic, so they couldn't have pets. This birthday she'd had no real hopes for anything she wanted. In fact she hadn't bothered to want anything much. There had been the card from her mother with twenty dollars in it, that was the main thing. Then, a blouse from Walt and Alice Everett, a bottle of bubble bath from Lori, and from Walt Junior a video game that he wanted himself. Lori would use the bubble bath, Walt Junior would play with the video game, and the blouse didn't go with any of her skirts. Another wonderful birthday.

The Everetts were stuck with her and they had to give her birthday presents, but they didn't put any effort into thinking what she might really want. They went through the motions, like they did everything else that they had to do for her because they were stuck with her.

Addie's legs ached behind the knees from squatting so long, so she stood up and hunched through the rest of the culvert and continued her upstream walk, past the Allens' house on her right and a gooseberry thicket on her left. The three hunting dogs lined up to watch her through their chain-link fence: Rosie the German Shorthair Pointer, Duke the yellow Lab, and Idiot the Springer Spaniel.

Mr. Allen also had guns and orange hunting vests and hats and hunting magazines and a four-wheel-drive Bronco. He just never found the time to go hunting. The dogs lived their lives in a ten-by-twelve concrete run and the guns stayed in their racks. Addie thought Mr. Allen was crazy, but then she thought that about a lot of adults.

She used to make plans to sneak over some night and let the dogs out and take them for a wonderful run through the fields and woods, and then they would love her deeply and dearly and forever, for giving them what they wanted most. But she never did it. The dream was wonderful, but when it came down to doing it, she was afraid they would get away from her and get killed on the highway.

Beyond the Allens' backyard Addie was in new territory. Off to her left she could see familiar buildings and a slice of the highway, and over her right shoulder she could see the backs of the houses of town, houses whose fronts were as familiar to her as her own face. But she had never before been in this exact spot, seeing her world from this viewpoint.

She ducked under a barbed-wire fence and plodded on, along the edge of a cornfield where the creek was lined by only a sheer edging of saplings. As she walked, an old childish excitement began to bubble up in her, the excitement of possibility. *Something* might happen. She was in a new place, doing a strange thing, and it was her birthday after all. It was possible that her angel had something in store for her.

Her angel. She smiled at herself. That was an old fantasy, surely outgrown by now. Or . . . maybe not. It was just an idea that had come to her several years ago, after her mother had dumped her on the Everetts. The idea was that everyone had a ghost, an angel, a spirit, whatever, who was assigned to them, to be with them all the time and just take an interest in their lives.

Addie didn't think of hers as a guardian angel since she wasn't conscious of dangers in her life. And it wasn't exactly an imaginary friend either, because that would have been another child like herself. No, her angel was more like some sort of big, pillowy adult who was overflowing with kindness and wisdom and warm laughter, but without any trace of scolding, punishing, even thinking anything bad about Addie.

She crawled through another wire fence and found herself in another pasture. This one was hilly, being closer to the range of rocky bluffs ahead. Granite boulders pierced the turf and made cliffs and caves on either side of the creek. Just ahead was one such rocky hillside blocking her view and forcing the creek to curve sharply away to the right. Between the rock wall and the creek bed was a patch of grass and ferns and small purple and white flowers.

It was too pretty a place to wade past, so Addie sloshed up onto the bank and lay down on her back, her fingers laced behind her head.

"Okay now," she said to her angel, "here I am. Here I am in this magical glen, and I'm unhappy. Now is the time you're supposed to do something. Turn yourself into a fairy godmother with one of those little sticks with a star on the end of it that make wishes come true.

"Or no, I've got a better idea. Turn yourself into one of those Irish things, those little elf things in curly shoes, that will lead me to the secret door in the mountain, and through the door is this magical world under the earth, where children never grow up or have to go to school or do anything they don't want to do."

The afternoon was still except for the small sounds of a cardinal hopping and fussing at her from the branch of a tree across the creek, the rippling sound of the water itself, which she could hear now that she wasn't splashing in it, and occasionally, far off, car sounds from the highway.

Nothing was going to happen. Of course, Addie knew that. She never really believed anything was going to happen just because she *wanted* it so hurtfully badly. She'd always wanted secret things hurtfully badly, and the wanting had never been enough to make them come true. She knew that by now.

She knew there were no such things as personal angels and fairy godmothers and secret doors in the mountainsides, but she hated knowing it. She didn't want to know it.

She heard a soft swishing in the grass, caught a flash of white at the corner of her vision. She sat up feeling momentarily dizzy and disoriented, as though she might have dozed off, might still be asleep.

On the far side of the creek but startlingly close to her stood a pony. He had just lowered his head

to graze when he saw her, and his head was still
low as he studied her.

Their eyes were level, staring at one another
across the sparkling ribbon of the creek. Within
Addie stirred a wild and childish hope.

This was it. This was her angel incarnate.

2

"It's just a pony," Addie told herself sternly, but a deep part of her didn't believe it.

He was white, a clear blue white except for his knees where gray smudges showed, as though he had knelt in dust. His muzzle was blue-gray skin, his eyes almost black against the white face, and huge— huge eyes fringed with lashes so long and white they made Addie smile.

He was a large pony, fat and plushy in spite of the slickness of his coat. His back sank in a soft downward curve from shoulders to hips, like a hammock, inviting. He wore no halter, no mark of civilization that would have proclaimed his reality.

Slowly Addie stood up. The pony lifted his head as she rose, so that his eyes remained level with hers. He watched her mildly but didn't move away.

"I'm Addie Harvey. Who are you?" She extended her hand toward him, offering herself to him. Barely looking down, she stepped into the creek, took two liquid steps and rose on the other side, within touching distance now of her pony.

She had never been so close to a horse. Horses seen from car windows or in Memorial Day parades in Stevens Point, that was as close as she had been, so far. There were girls Addie knew who worshiped horses, drew pictures of them and read books about them; some of them even had horses of their own. Addie hadn't shared their passion.

She could have. The longings were there, but they were buried under more pressing hungers for a human loving touch. And she shied away from openly sharing horse-love with the girls at school because it would have made a bond between them and her. Something in her warned Addie away from that. She was different from the rest of them and she knew it, even if they didn't. If she allowed friendships to form, they would find out what it was about Addie that was so bad her own mother gave her away. Addie herself didn't know what it was, but she knew it had to be there, and she didn't want to make friends only to lose them. It hurt too much.

So she didn't draw horse heads on her school notebooks and she didn't read *Misty of Chinco-*

teague. But now her fingertips were close to a horse's muzzle, close enough to feel the warm, damp puffs from his nostrils, and with an almost physical pain the crust in Addie began to crack. Love came up in her as hot and forceful as molten lava rising in an old volcano.

She moved closer but left the first touching up to him. Whiskers brushed her palm, then suede-soft, rubbery lips. She shivered.

His head was long, as long as her arm almost. Slowly it moved toward her body, his one nearside eye fastened on hers. She had never seen so big an eye, a liquid black ball with an odd violet oval for the iris. The oval expanded as his head moved into the shadow of her body. A cluster of three or four hairs several inches long grew from an eyebrow spot just above the eye, and another such cluster grew from a spot beneath his jaw. Her hand came up and stroked the long, long bones of his underjaw and the flat round plate-like bones at the sides of his face.

He lifted his muzzle and brought it close to her face and made puffs of his breath. She breathed in his air; he breathed in hers. An exchange of trust passed between them. He was hers then. They both knew it.

Her hands explored him; the harsh waves of

his mane and the oven-warm place under it between the fall of mane and the hard slickness of neck. She traced the long ridges of his shoulder bone, the grooves and planes of his foreleg. Her palms followed the down curve of his back and its rise toward his hips. She found the valley along his spine where his fat rose up on either side, and the roll of fat above the root of his tail.

She explored the length of his tail and found a bone within the fall of hair. She smiled at herself for having supposed a horse's tail was only hair. She bent over and looked under his belly to see that he was male. She'd known he was anyway. She'd known that instinctively.

The pony lowered his head and began moving it in slow arcs from side to side, nipping at the grass. For some time Addie stood beside him with her arm across his back, pressing her ribs against his and stroking his far side with her open palm.

There was more to do. The important part. She felt her arm across his back and knew it must be her legs that gripped his sides. He must carry her. He must be big and strong and bear her away over the fields. He must have the power of his greater strength over her and yet do her bidding. He must have the power to hurt her but choose not to.

Then she would be loved.

These thoughts were not clear in her mind, but the feelings were powerful within her and she knew she would ride him.

She stood beside him and jumped and tried to throw her body far enough across his back to wriggle up from there, but he was too tall and too round. He lifted his head from his grazing but didn't move away.

"You'll have to help me," Addie said. Placing her hands flat on the sides of his face and coaxing him with her voice, she led him a few steps to the left to a place where the ground sloped and she could stand a bit higher. But it wasn't enough. She flung herself at him three times and slid down each time.

"You'll have to help me," she said again, looking into the purple slit in his eye.

He left her then and walked along the creek bed to a sandy place in a curve of the creek. With great deliberation he lowered himself to the ground and rolled over onto his back, kicking his four legs in the ecstasy of the itch relieved and showing his blue gray belly to the world.

He rolled again, so that he was lying doglike, with his legs tucked under him, his back invitingly

15

exposed to Addie. He paused, and in that instant she accepted his invitation. She ran and straddled his back and fastened her fists in his mane as he rose with a heave and a lurch, bearing her upward with him. In that instant a belief was born in Addie that no amount of logic would ever displace, a belief that this pony had been sent to her to give her what she needed, to be for her what no human being had been.

He lowered his head and splayed his four legs out and shook himself as a wet dog shakes. It was a quick, violent movement that tossed Addie clear of contact with his back, yet kept her somehow balanced so that she was still astride when his shaking ceased.

She laughed aloud, realizing she was on his back and unafraid. "Carry me away," she sang to him and gripped him with her legs. The hammock shape of his body carried hers securely. Her knees pressed into cushions of fat. She stroked his neck with one hand but kept the other locked in his mane.

He walked forward. "Carry me away," she commanded again, and he did. As her heels dug into him for grip he rocked forward in a slow, smooth lope that enchanted Addie with its rhythm. Trees and grass and boulders passed her vision and the sun-warmed wind brushed her face, but she made no effort to control the pony. This was his magical journey; she was his passenger and his charge.

They followed the winding creek bed among rock ledges and trees. The pony slowed where the footing was cluttered and picked his way cautiously among rocks and down embankments. Then in the open he cantered again, shaking his mane and blowing snorts of high pleasure. One snort sent drops of wetness flying back onto Addie's arm, and she laughed again and spanked his neck.

By that time they were in the open, heading toward the range of bluffs to the north, and a cluster of trees and buildings at the base of the bluffs.

"Whoa," Addie commanded. She didn't want to go close to the buildings. She didn't want her magical ride to be nothing more than a hungry animal's gallop toward food.

He slowed to a walk.

"Good boy. Now turn around and take me back to the creek." She pressed against the side of his neck and made him turn back the way they'd come. When they were hidden from the buildings by an outcropping of mossy rocks Addie commanded him to whoa again and with overwhelming reluctance slid to the ground.

17

The sight of the house had reminded her that her mystical friend was also a real live pony who belonged to some person. That person probably lived in the house she had glimpsed through the trees, and that person very probably didn't want strange girls sneaking into his pasture and stealing rides on his pony.

The thought rankled. Addie hated it. This was her pony in that deep place where souls met, and it was wrong that the actual real life ownership of this woolly form was in someone else's hands.

He was hers. She needed him to be hers legally, openly, in every way.

She thought about the twenty dollars of birthday money. She thought about the ease with which her mother always gave her money for school things and about the absent-minded willingness of Mrs. Everett to let Addie do what she wanted.

Buying a pony might be possible.

Yes. Why not possible? Yes, of course. He was supposed to be hers, and he would be.

She waded into the creek and squatted in the water, washing off the dirt marks and white hairs on the insides of her legs, evidence of her stolen ride. Then, on shoes that squished with each step, she set out to walk across the pasture toward the distant buildings. The pony fell into step behind her, so close his breath puffed damply against the cotton of her shirt.

Once she stopped and went back to the pony's side to scrub with her fingertips the indentation of her legs in his coat. They walked on side by side after that, with him slightly leading the way, Addie following with her arm thrown companionably across his neck.

As they approached, the details of the buildings emerged: a tiny, red barn with half-doors that had white Z-shaped boards bracing them; a house built of limestone blocks, its doors and windows set deep in the thickness of the walls. Pines circled the house but were held back from the lawn by a curve of stone wall.

A red plank fence made a small paddock beside the barn. Its gate stood open to the pasture, and within it a double door stood open to the pony's stall. Someone leaned against the fence—a woman, Addie saw. Her arms were folded on the top plank and her face was turned toward Addie and the pony, watching them.

Addie was afraid. She had never before been

especially timid of adults, but then never before had they held such power over her happiness as did this strange woman, this owner of Addie's pony.

She straightened herself and dropped her arm from the pony's neck and made herself ready.

3

Stepping toward the woman over the hoof-chopped earth near the barn, Addie had time to register impressions, a warrior sizing up the enemy.

The woman was very tall, somewhat thickened through the middle, but with broad shoulders and long neck, so that her weight was carried proudly and diminished by the straightness of her back. Her face was broad and strong featured, lined and weathered and heavy browed. Streaked gray hair was pulled back into a figure eight–shaped knot at her neck, elegant in spite of escaped strands about her ears.

Addie had never known a woman with long hair knotted at the back like that; she found it intimidating. The women in Addie's life wore their hair short, mostly curled into shapelessness at the Kut and Kurl Beauty Shop in the blue house next door to the post

21

office. Addie's mother's hair was long but loose, not queenly like this woman's.

She wore brown denim slacks with elastic at the waist, a white blouse open at the neck and sleeveless. The skin of her neck and upper arms was browned but hung with tiny crepey wrinkles, as though she had shrunk within it. On one knuckly, veiny hand she wore a large, diamond-cluster ring, further proclaiming that she was a personage above Addie's level.

Addie stopped in front of her and tried to think of the right thing to say. The pony paused there too and leaned his head against the woman to rub his itchy face against her blouse. Jealousy shot through Addie. "Is that your pony?" she asked, because something had to be said.

The woman's voice was neither warm nor cold, but strong, gravelly. "Yes. My daughter's pony. Madeline's pony. Who are you?"

"Addie Harvey. I live over there with the Everetts."

The woman's eyes fastened on Addie. "Oh yes. You're that one."

The pony moved away to a crude wooden shelf built low on the barn wall to hold a block of mineral salt. The salt block was pink and rounded out of its square shape by pony tongue. He licked it now, running his long tongue over it and over it, and ending by scraping it with his teeth as though the licking wasn't fast enough.

Addie stood up onto the fence and the woman turned her back to it, so that they were both looking toward the pony.

"What's his name?"

"Ribbon. Chief Ribbon Raider, in his young years, but we called him Ribbon. What were you doing in my pasture?"

"Exploring." Addie relaxed a few degrees, sensing that the woman wanted to talk and was not angry at the trespass. "It's my birthday, and I wanted to go up the creek to see where it went. It goes through our backyard," she added, as though the connection of the creek between them was enough. "Ribbon," she added, liking the sound of it. "Did you have him a long time?" Addie asked. Already in her mind the woman's ownership of Ribbon was coming to an end.

"Yes. A long time. Most of his life. He'll be thirty next spring."

Addie sucked in her breath. "I didn't know ponies could live that long."

The woman seemed to be talking to herself,

over Addie's head. "He was a five-year-old when Mr. Portree and I brought him here from Virginia. He is a purebred Connemara, you know. A fine Junior Hunter in his day. A fine pony. There were none of his quality in the Midwest, you know. We had to go back to my home, in Virginia, to find a pony good enough for Madeline."

For a flashing second Addie heard how that statement would sound to the Everetts, to the other people she knew around Amherst who loved their Wisconsin so fiercely, so glowingly. It came to her in that flash that this woman was an outsider in Amherst too, like Addie. Who around here could like a woman who looked down her nose at Amherst?

"What's a Junior Hunter?"

The woman didn't answer.

"Mrs. Portree?" Addie guessed that was her name, assuming Mr. Portree was her husband.

The woman stood away from the fence and walked across the paddock and through a gate at the far side. Addie stood uncertainly, waiting for a cue. At the gate the woman turned her eyes to Addie and motioned with her head toward the house.

Wordlessly Addie followed.

The house had the cavelike coolness of thick

stone walls and a smell of wax and honey. Plank floors and the polished surfaces of furniture gleamed where the sun slanted through the windows. It was the living room that they entered, a long room with windows at the far end facing into the bluffs. A massive brick fireplace and its flanking bookshelves filled a long wall. Leather sofas, a grand piano with its top canted upward, and rugs woven of soft, creamy fabrics made the room rich and beautiful beyond any room Addie had ever seen. She breathed it in. She wanted to wrap her arms around it and bury herself in it forever. But the woman was there and she was the enemy, at least for now, until Ribbon belonged to Addie.

Mrs. Portree took a large, framed photograph from one of the bookshelves and handed it to Addie. The glare of daylight on the glass hid the picture until Addie tipped it to the right angle. She studied it, frowning in her concentration.

It was a picture of a girl and a pony flying over a three-rail length of fence that Addie recognized as a horse-show jump. But the pony was darker than Ribbon, a smoky gray with dapple rings on its sides and hips, and black legs. It wore a hornless English saddle and an English-looking bridle, and its mane was only a row of ribboned bumps up the length of its neck, so that it looked shaved. The girl's face was indistinct beneath a black velvet hunt cap. She wore a dark tailored jacket with tight pale breeches, and high, dark, shining boots. And gloves, expensive-looking leather gloves on her hands. Addie hated her for the clothes and the pony.

"That was Madeline on Ribbon, at the Chicago International. They placed fourth in Junior Hunter out of a field of thirty-two. Madeline was thirteen here."

Addie squinted and brought the picture closer to her face. "That can't be Ribbon. He's a different color. He's all white."

"Gray horses lighten with age. Ribbon was quite dark as a youngster. He would have been eight when this was taken."

Among the rows of books on the shelves were several other photographs of Ribbon and Madeline, and Mrs. Portree got them down one at a time and handed them to Addie. One showed Madeline and Ribbon standing in a line with a man and woman on tall, dark horses, each horse the proper size for its rider, with the girl and the gray pony at the end of the line. Addie stared for a long moment at that family group, sour envy in her stomach.

Another photograph showed Madeline and

Ribbon standing in a show ring, the girl holding a tall trophy in her arms and smiling into the camera, while a large purple rosette fluttered from the pony's bridle. Mrs. Portree nodded toward the trophy itself, where it stood on the mantle, and to the rosette which hung within a glassed frame on the opposite wall.

"Junior Hunter," Mrs. Portree said finally, "refers to the class and division in which a horse or pony is shown. Madeline's age classified them as Junior, you see, and Hunter meant that they showed over jumps and were judged on their ability over the jumps. Then, too, Ribbon's size put them in the pony division, ponies thirteen-two to fourteen-two hands high. You understand?"

Addie nodded although she didn't understand about the hands. She wanted to get the conversation to the important thing.

"Does Madeline still live here?" She looked around, dreading to see an elegant girl in riding boots and breeches come into the room.

"No, she's married now. She lives in Cleveland."

"Does your husband live here?"

"No, he's gone." Her voice became abrupt.

Addie veered away from that, assuming Mr. Portree must be dead and it was sad for Mrs. Portree to talk about him. "Then how come you kept Ribbon if Madeline grew up and got married? Didn't you want to sell him?"

"No."

The word came down like a cleaver into Addie's heart. It might not work, she realized with a wash of panic. She might not get him.

"Does Madeline come back to visit him sometimes?"

"Of course she does. She comes home to see me, and of course she wants to see her old pony. She loves Ribbon."

Through her lonely childhood Addie had developed an instinct for hearing tones as well as words, and her instinct told her there was something harsh and hollow here.

"Do you think you might ever sell him?" she prodded more carefully around the edge of Mrs. Portree's hardness.

"No. He is Madeline's pony."

"I was thinking about buying a pony," Addie ventured. "I got some money for my birthday and I was thinking about buying a pony. How much would one like Ribbon cost, do you think?"

Mrs. Portree snorted and moved through the room toward the front door, as though she were suddenly tired of Addie's company and wanted to be rid of her. "Not very much, a pony that old. He wouldn't have much value to anyone. He could die any time now. He's almost thirty."

"Would twenty dollars be enough?" She held her breath.

Mrs. Portree reached the door and held it open, obviously waiting for Addie to go through it and disappear. "I've told you, Ribbon is not for sale. I'm not going to talk prices with you, girl."

On the worn stone entrance step, Addie hesitated and turned back to look up at Mrs. Portree's face. It looked wooden against the dark interior of the house.

"Could I come back and visit Ribbon some time? If I don't make a nuisance of myself?"

Mrs. Portree's face warmed then. She didn't smile but her eyes softened, and she said, "I expect."

"Could I ride him some time?"

"I don't know. We'll see."

We'll see. The classic evasion. But it would have to do for now. Addie turned and ran across the grass toward the pasture and home, unaware that the dirt rim on the seat of her shorts betrayed the fact that the requested ride had already been stolen.

4

Addie was used to keeping her thoughts private in the Everetts' house, so keeping her pony dreams to herself that evening was no trick.

All through supper Walt Junior argued for permission to play an instrument in the school band when he started fourth grade in a few weeks, and Lori provided a counterpoint whine about something she wanted to do or didn't want to do. Addie tuned out both of them and listened only to the plans billowing in her mind.

Owning Ribbon. That was the thing. Once he belonged to her then she would be loved forever. That thought wasn't clear in her mind, but her feelings swirled around it and built on it and exposed glimpses of it now and then. Owning Ribbon would fix everything that was wrong in her life.

So. First, permission from the Everetts, then

money from Mother so Addie could approach Mrs. Portree with at least fifty dollars to offer. That was the way the thing would have to be done. And then, tackle Mrs. Portree again with money and permission in hand and a serious offer to make.

The two biggest problems—where to keep Ribbon and what to do about Madeline's not wanting to let go of her pony—solved each other some time during supper when it occurred to Addie that she could keep Ribbon right where he was. It was close enough that Addie could run over every morning before school and every afternoon after school, and love him and take care of him. Madeline wouldn't even need to know about it. Ribbon would still be there when she came home for visits, and then Addie would just be a neighbor girl who came to pet him.

Privately Addie didn't feel that Madeline had any claim on Ribbon, not if she would move away and leave him. If Ribbon lived long enough for Addie to grow up and move away, she would most certainly take him with her. Anybody who didn't love him enough to do that didn't deserve him.

After supper the rest of the family wandered out into the warm lingering evening while Addie started on the dishes. She'd begun volunteering for the supper dishes recently, thinking that Alice

Everett's gratitude would warm into something more, that Alice or Big Walt would look in on Addie doing her solitary chores in the glare of the kitchen light and be moved by the sight of her. Cinderella grubbing uncomplainingly while the ugly step-children loafed.

It didn't work out that way, though. Alice was grateful at first and then just began to assume Addie would take care of the dishes. Big Walt never seemed to notice things like who did what around the house. He just came home in the evenings and told jokes he'd heard at work that day, at the box factory in Stevens Point. He'd give Alice a smootch and pat the mound of her stomach where the new baby was growing, and he'd wrestle with Walt Junior and look at whatever Lori showed him and say, "How's it going, Ad?" and that was about all he ever noticed of her.

Tonight Addie didn't resent the fact that no one came into the kitchen to see her working away all by herself. Her vision was full of Ribbon, her body was full of the feel of him carrying her over the grass, his mane like silver wires in her fist and his body like warm plush against her bare legs.

As soon as he was hers, they would go riding up the highway, right through Amherst, past the post office and the bank and the grocery store, where everyone in town would see them. Then Addie Harvey wouldn't be just that little girl the Everetts got stuck with. She would be Miss Adrian Harvey, horsewoman.

The dream focused into a close-up shot of Adrian Harvey in black boots and velvet hunt cap and tight pale breeches, sailing over the jump at the horse show. No. She erased that one. She didn't want to be Madeline. She didn't want to make Ribbon do artificial things like that. She just wanted to be alone with him in grassy fields.

And behind the main pictures in her head, like shadow images on the television screen during bad weather, was a picture of a family group—father, mother, and Addie—all on their horses and smiling their happiness at the camera.

After the last dish was put away and the counter tops wiped off, Addie turned out the light and went out onto the screened-in porch off the kitchen. This was her summer bedroom, this porch with the fold-away cot along one end and a rag rug on the painted floor boards, and screens all around.

In the winter she had to double up with Lori, and both of them hated that. Lori was seven now and fiercely possessive of her things and her territory. Addie would have felt that way, too, had she ever had territory that seemed hers.

Addie didn't turn her light on; she only wanted to check the box under her cot, to be sure the twenty dollars was still there with the birthday card from her mother. It was. She sat on the cot to think about money for a minute, to do some figuring in her head about how much to ask Mother for, and when to do it. But then she heard Alice and Big Walt talking just beyond the screen and knew they were talking about her. They didn't say her name, but their voices took on a special tone that Addie recognized and hated.

The screen porch was at the side of the house but the front edge of it was close to an unscreened porch at the front of the house, and that was where Alice and Big Walt sat talking.

Big Walt's voice had almost the same whine Walt Junior's had when he argued, except in a deeper tone. "It isn't just the crib, honey, you know that. It's all the other stuff a baby needs, the play-pen and walker and bath junk, all that equipment. There's no way we can squeeze all that in with Lori *and* Addie."

"I know that," Alice said in her old, tired voice. "Why do you think I've been at you all summer to enclose the screen porch and make a year-round room out of it?"

"Yes, and like I said a million times already, even doing the work myself, that would cost a good two or three thousand just for lumber and insulation and some kind of heating system. When I thought I was going to get the overtime, we could have swung it, but with Charmin canceling their contract . . ."

"I know," Alice sighed.

Addie hated it! She hated being here in this family causing problems for them. She hated not being able to do anything about it, and she hated them for making her feel this way.

Walt's voice got harder. "Honey, I know we've talked about this before, and I know you don't want to do it, but you're just going to have to have it out with Gloria. There's no sense in this. There's no reason on God's green earth why we should be taking care of her kid all these years."

"There were reasons . . ."

"Oh yeah, at first maybe. She falls in love with some jerk who doesn't like kids, so she dumps Addie on us just till she gets him to marry her. Just for the summer, she says, so we do it. Honey, Alice, my love, we never intended to sign on for the lifetime job of raising your old school friend's kid."

"I know it." Alice sounded miserable. "I know it's dragged on a little longer than we counted on . . ."

"Seven years," he said drily.

"I know. But you know Gloria, honey. She's just one of those people that it's hard to say no to."

"She's a user," Walt snapped. "She's a perfect example of the tyranny of the weak. She goes around looking like some sort of fading flower of womanhood and somehow manages to coast along all through her life manipulating other people into doing her dirty work."

"That's not true," Alice said, but she didn't sound very sure.

"Yes it is. She got pregnant with Addie in the first place because she was too lazy to get a job after she and Jerry got married, you know that as well as I do. And then after he took off, she was too lazy to get up on her hind legs and support herself and Addie, so she glommed onto the first man that came down the pike, who turned out to be a bigger jerk than Jerry."

"Well, that's for sure," Alice admitted.

"Okay, I can see all that. Maybe. And I can see you offering to take Addie for a little while till that marriage got off the ground. But honey, seven years? Come on. I mean, this is ridiculous."

"The money comes in handy," Alice argued weakly.

"Oh sure, what, sixty, sixty-five a month. It costs us more than that to feed Addie and buy her clothes and school stuff, you know that. We don't even break even, money-wise."

"What if I asked her to raise it? Maybe a hundred a month?"

"Allie, look. Read my lips. You aren't listening to what I'm saying here. This house is not big enough for three children of our own, plus waifs and strays."

"Addie's not . . ."

"Oh, I know it. I didn't mean it that way. Heck, I like Addie, too, hon. She's a nice, quiet kid. I'm not saying anything against Addie personally, but just . . ."

"I know. She really isn't our responsibility. And you're right, things are going to be crowded as heck around here after little Jason-Angela gets here. But we can't very well kick Addie out into the street, can we? And she is a help around the place."

"I know. She tries. Like I said, Allie, it's nothing against the kid. I like her. But enough is enough. You know darn well Gloria will go right on taking advantage of us as long as we let her. Now is the time to put an end to it. Just tell her we aren't going to have room for Addie any more, because of the baby coming. Just tell her that."

Alice blew out a long sigh. "I'll think about it, okay?"

"Well don't think too long. Jason-Angela is getting anxious to get out of there, aren't you, baby? There, he kicked my hand. Did you feel that? He kicks like a boy."

Their voices got lower as they centered their attention around themselves, the three of them who were a real family.

Addie shivered and wrapped her arms around herself in a bleak hug.

She lay back on the cot, staring up at the narrow, brown boards of the porch ceiling, and thought about what to do now. She didn't dare ask Alice for permission to buy Ribbon. Not now. It would force Alice to tell her that she might have to move back with her mother.

This time yesterday the possibility of living with her mother would have excited her. Now all she could think of was Ribbon and the fifteen miles of unbridgeable distance between Ribbon and her mother's home in Stevens Point.

Impossible, impossible.

Maybe if I start doing the cooking, too, and washing all the dishes, not just supper. Maybe they'd decide they really do need me around here then.

She rolled over and punched the cot mattress again and again, but it didn't help. It didn't even make her tired enough to go to sleep.

She lay there, damp-eyed, needing Ribbon to love her and carry her away.

5

The next day was Thursday, grocery day because the Super Valu in Stevens Point gave double coupons on Thursdays. Addie's urge was to spend the day with Ribbon, but she knew she had to see her mother, and the weekly shopping trip was the best way to do that.

They had to leave right after breakfast in order to be back in time for Alice to watch "General Hospital." It would mean getting to her mother's before nine, and Addie knew that wasn't ideal because that early there was always the risk that Dutch might still be around. Dutch drove a delivery truck for Miller Brewing Company, and most of his customers were bars that didn't open very early in the day, so sometimes he was still at home when Addie got there. But it was a chance she had to take.

Dutch didn't like her. He didn't like kids in general, but Addie felt more hate from him than just that. It had to do with owning her mother, somehow. Dutch owned her mother and he didn't allow her to have friends or family except himself. Addie didn't know this in any concrete, provable way, but she knew it in the deep part of her that heard what wasn't said between people.

When she was younger, Addie used to study Dutch on the rare occasions when they were together. She tried to see what it was about him that was better than anything she was herself. He had to be better than she was, more valuable to her mother, because it was clear that a choice had been made, and Addie had been given away so that Gloria could keep Dutch.

He was a short, thick man with a bald head and his sweat smelled like the beer he drank and sold. He had a heavy face and heavy footsteps and his lips never lifted but curled downward arrogantly, even when he made his grimacing smile. She tried and tried to understand why her mother had given her away in exchange for this man, but she never could, and after a while she quit trying.

All through the drive from Amherst to Stevens

41

Point Addie sat in her usual place in the backseat with Walt Junior, elbow on the armrest, face close to the window, watching the familiar countryside roll past. She rehearsed what she would say to her mother about Ribbon. That part shouldn't be too hard. But she'd also have to get her mother to promise Alice more money for taking care of her. Otherwise they'd throw her out and she'd have to live where she couldn't be close to Ribbon. That was what squeezed her heart.

At the edge of town Alice turned off onto Valley Crest, then nosed the car into the driveway of Valley Crest Mobile Home Park. She didn't drive all the way to the blue trailer fourth on the left, and Addie was glad. She bore down on the door handle and stepped out as soon as the car stopped.

"I'll be back in about an hour," Alice said, and drove away.

Cautiously Addie peered up the drive toward the blue trailer. Whew. Dutch's beer truck was gone. She started up the row, feeling optimistic.

It was a pretty trailer park, Addie thought. The trailers sat angled in a herringbone pattern along the central driveway, like multicolored leaves on a branch. Each one had its little square of grass and its white-and-green metal storage shed behind. Several had miniature picket fences along flower borders. There were no children allowed here, not to live anyway.

Pine trees edged the park, and beyond the pines open fields rolled away on two sides. On the other two sides were new houses. Addie used to dream about living here, but just with her mother, not with Dutch. Or, just with her mother and her real father, whom she imagined to be nice although her mother had never wanted to tell Addie much about him.

She went up the metal steps, opened the screen door and knocked on the quilted blue metal of the inside door. Her mother opened it.

She was small and dark-haired like Addie, but her hair was long and wavy and beautiful. She'd started bleaching yellow streaks in it around her face, and they made her look different. She was wearing a blue flowery robe but her face was in place already, blue and silver eye shadow and black liner around her eyes and sparkly pink lipstick.

Gloria waved Addie into the trailer and said, "Hi sugar, what brings you to town this morning? Come on in, have a cup of coffee with me. Oh that's right, you don't drink it yet, do you? I've got some diet Pepsi, okay? Whew, I just can't seem to get in gear this morning."

On her way to the refrigerator Gloria clicked off the radio's rock music. At the front end of the trailer was a table with a bench curving all around it. Addie slid in and accepted the can of cold Pepsi. It was too early in the morning for her stomach to want the acid of the pop, but her mother kept forgetting that from one visit to the next. She always offered pop and by now Addie had given up on explaining and just took the can.

"Thanks for the birthday card and money," she said as Gloria eased into her spot in the booth and gathered in her coffee mug, ashtray, lighter, and pack of cigarettes.

Gloria lit up and aimed a stream of smoke away from Addie's face. It drifted back. "Did you have a nice birthday, sugar? Just think, thirteen years old. Doesn't that seem *old*? My God, I can't believe I'm the mother of a teenager. Who'd think it, to look at me? About time for you to start having boyfriends, huh, baby? First thing we know, you'll be getting married."

"That would solve everybody's problem," Addie said drily.

44

Gloria focused on her then. "What's that supposed to mean?"

Addie shrugged. "It's getting kind of crowded there, Mom, with the new baby coming and everything. Alice and Walt want to fix up the screen porch to make another room, but they can't afford it. Do you think you could pay them more for my keep?"

Jump right in, get the worst part over.

Gloria frowned and blew a river of smoke up toward the top of the refrigerator. "I don't know, sugar. I'd have to talk to Dutch about that. Maybe. We might be able to swing a little more."

Mentally holding her breath, Addie plunged on. "They might ask you to take me back here to live. You wouldn't be able to do that, probably, huh?"

"Aw, sugar." Gloria reached across the table and squeezed Addie's wrist. "I'd give anything if I could have you here with me, you know that, don't you?"

Anything but Dutch, Addie thought, but she nodded, giving Gloria the answer she wanted.

"Listen, you're growing up, you're getting old enough to understand how it is with women. I need to have a man in my life. You can understand that,

45

can't you, darling? Unfortunately, my man happens to be one of those who is very possessive. He doesn't want me to love anybody but him. He gets mad if I even talk to my girlfriends on the phone when he's home. It just wouldn't work out, trying to squeeze you into this little old trailer with Dutch."

Addie nodded, relieved.

"It's not always going to be like this, though, I promise you. We're saving up for the down payment on a house over in Crestview Heights, and when we get that, then maybe I'll be able to bring Dutch around about having you come live with us. I keep working on him all the time, you know that. I want to have my little girl with me."

There had been a time when those words had sent Addie weeping and clinging to Gloria. They didn't work any more though. Addie could see too much truth between the words.

But it was all right, now that she had Ribbon.

"Mom?"

"What, sugar?"

"There's this pony. I want to buy him. This woman that has him, he was her daughter's but the daughter grew up and moved away, so she doesn't need him any more, and she lives just up the road from the Everetts so I could keep him at her place.

And he's real old, almost thirty, so he wouldn't cost very much to buy."

Gloria reached toward the tiny television set on the shelf behind the booth and snapped it on. "The Price Is Right" was just about to start. Addie knew it was one of her mother's favorite programs and that she never missed it if she could help it.

Swiftly Addie said, "He probably wouldn't cost more than about another thirty dollars along with the twenty you gave me for my birthday. And then maybe ten or fifteen a month for his feed. Do you think you could help me out with that much? I'm old enough now to start getting some baby-sitting jobs pretty soon, so I'll be able to pay for his feed if you could just help me get started. Could you, Mom?"

Gloria ground out her cigarette in the overflowing ashtray and focused on her daughter again. The commercials were still on; the program hadn't started yet. "A pony? Is it a gentle one? I wouldn't want you getting hurt."

Addie expanded with the excitement of talking about her love. "He's very gentle. I rode him already, without a saddle or bridle or anything, and he just carried me wherever I wanted to go. And he's a purebred Con-something, and he used to be a show pony. A jumper. But now he's real quiet and gentle because he's so old. He's pure white, Mom, except for gray knees, and he's got big dark eyes and long eyelashes and a long mane and tail. He's just beautiful. His name is Ribbon."

Gloria smiled and got her checkbook down from her purse on top of the refrigerator. "Well, we'll just call it a little extra birthday present, shall we? Don't say anything about it in front of Dutch though, okay? I'll put this down in the checkbook as 'school supplies for Addie.' "

She ripped out the check and handed it to Addie, who folded it reverently and buttoned it into the hip pocket of her shorts.

"Thanks, Mom."

"I wish I could do more for you, sugar." Gloria looked down into Addie's eyes with a great and genuine sadness, and for the first time Addie understood that her mother was in some ways a victim, too.

"I know. It's okay." She comforted Gloria as best she could, then they turned together to watch "The Price Is Right." They had a contest between themselves to see who could win the most by the end of the program.

6

That afternoon Addie walked the long way around, by the road, to find Mrs. Portree's house. She felt that this visit was too important to risk getting there by trespassing through the pasture.

Her eyes were hungry for Ribbon, whom she saw as a white flash among the trees beyond the barn, but she marched up the stone path toward the front door, determined to tackle the important part first.

No one answered her knock. Her hopes sank. She had wrapped herself in courage and rolled her money into a wad in her jeans pocket; the moment was now. But if Mrs. Portree wasn't home . . . Somehow Addie had not thought of that possibility. She had imagined Mrs. Portree to be as solitary in Amherst as Addie herself was, and the thought that the woman might be out visiting friends struck Addie as a kind of betrayal.

But there she was, coming around the corner of the house in dirt-stained slacks, with a weeding claw in one hand and a fistful of creeping charlie in the other.

"I thought I heard someone. It's you again." Mrs. Portree's voice sounded neither angry nor welcoming.

Addie was so relieved to find her at home that she plunged in without a warm-up.

"I got money from my Mom to buy Ribbon. Will you sell him to me?"

The woman looked down at Addie from a great height.

"No."

"But I *want* him."

"Then *want* shall be your master."

"What?"

Mrs. Portree walked to a wheelbarrow and tossed the weeds into it. She lay the tool atop the heap of drying weeds and turned to look at Addie again, fists on hips.

"Why did you bother coming out here again? Why did you get money from your mother when I told you yesterday I would never sell my daughter's pony?"

"But if you only knew how much I wanted him . . ." Addie fought tears of anger and frustration.

Again, as it had the day before, Mrs. Portree's face softened around the eyes. "Why? Why do you have to have this particular pony? Go find yourself another one that is for sale. Go find one that's young enough to give you some use."

Addie could only shake her head. "It has to be Ribbon. I love him."

The woman snorted. "You saw him one time in the pasture. And stole a ride on him." She leveled a hard look at Addie and dared her to lie.

Addie looked down at the grass. "I just sat on him for a few minutes. I didn't think anybody'd mind." She forced herself to go on, past her own protective barriers. "I don't have many friends around here, and Ribbon just seemed like . . . I don't know . . . he was special. Like he liked me."

Mrs. Portree looked away then, out at some distant point across the valley, and Addie sensed that she was thinking of something in her own life. The woman began to walk toward the barn, and Addie fell into step beside her.

51

"I won't sell him to you. But you can see him."

"Could I ride him?"

Again that hard look shafted down from Mrs. Portree's eyes. "Do you know how? Have you had lessons?"

"Lessons? To ride a pony? Do you need lessons for that?"

Mrs. Portree sighed. "Not the way children around here do it, I don't suppose. But to ride correctly, as we did back where I came from, you most certainly need lessons."

Addie was torn, but only for a flash. She didn't want lessons, didn't want riding Ribbon to be anything but a natural and magical happening between the two of them. But it was a way to get close to Mrs. Portree.

"Would you give me lessons?"

They were at the paddock gate. Mrs. Portree didn't answer but looked again at Addie, more thoroughly this time, as she held the gate open. She reached into the barn for an apple from a row of apples on a crossbeam. Standing in the open door of Ribbon's stall, she called, "Hoo-eee Ribbon."

The pale form in the trees stirred and moved slowly out into the sunlight. The pony didn't come quickly, or even directly, but made his way toward them eating a snatch of grass with each step.

While she waited, Addie glanced around at his stall, smelled the cleanness of the straw underfoot. It occurred to her that this woman had been doing a lot of work, for years and years, just to take care of this pony. Twenty years probably, since Madeline grew up and moved away. Addie wasn't old enough to imagine doing any one thing for twenty years, much less caring for an outgrown pony. Even if it did belong to a daughter she loved, still that was an immense lot of feed-carrying and manure-shoveling. Addie quaked at the meaning of that thought, at the love it must represent.

In that instant she began to know that she would not win this battle. No matter how much she wanted Ribbon, it was possible that she wasn't going to get him.

She blinked the moistness from her eyes and deliberately stared toward the sunlight to give her eyes a reason for tearing up. Ribbon walked into her vision then, her dear Ribbon, with a wisp of grass still hanging from one corner of his mouth.

She went to him and wrapped her arms around his neck and leaned into him. Something tapped her on the shoulder; it was the apple, in Mrs. Portree's hand. Addie took it and offered it to Ribbon.

"No no, on the flat of your hand. Get your fingers out of his way, girl. He won't want to bite you, but you must give him a chance. He can't get at the apple if your fingers are wrapped around it."

"Like this?"

"Yes, that's it."

Ribbon's lips drew in the apple, his jaws bore down on it until apple juice dripped onto Addie's palm. She giggled and wiped her hand on her hip.

"I doubt that his saddle will fit him any more," Mrs. Portree said from within the barn. "He's gotten so swaybacked these past few years, I'm afraid the saddle would rub sores on his withers."

Addie led Ribbon into the barn and stood beside him, watching Mrs. Portree sort through dusty tack that hung on the wall just outside the stall. Although the woman still had not smiled, nor anything close to it, Addie knew from the way she moved that Mrs. Portree was enjoying herself.

"At least his bridle will still fit." Mrs. Portree came into the stall wiping at the bridle with the tail of her blouse. "And the saddle isn't important. You'll learn balance more quickly without it. One thing— what did you say your name was?"

"Addie. Harvey."

"Yes. One thing, Addie, this pony is not to be run. Do you understand me? He is very old, and much too fat, and completely out of condition. A hard gallop in this weather could kill him. I won't have him abused. If you start riding him regularly then probably later on he'll be able to do some easy cantering, when he gets muscled up a little, but not until I say so."

Addie nodded.

The woman shot Addie another barbed look. "Are you honest? Can I trust you?"

Addie looked her back as straight as she could and said, "I'm not always honest but I would never do anything to hurt Ribbon."

Slowly Mrs. Portree's face shifted and broke and bent into a smile. Her skin seemed to fight the pull of the muscles, as though it were being forced where it could not go.

"Good enough, then, Addie Harvey. Here is your bridle. Hold it by the crown, in your right hand, cradle the bit in your left palm—no, like this. That's it. Gently over the ears. Always handle a horse's ears as if they were delicate birds in your hand. There now, buckle the throatlatch, not too tight, loose enough so you can slip your hand in

55

under it. Good. Now bring him along out here and I'll give you a knee up."

With breath-catching joy Addie settled once again into the cradle of Ribbon's back. Mrs. Portree's instructions were hardly a shadow on Addie's light spirit as Ribbon carried her out the paddock gate and up the lawn toward the house. In front of her, his thick white ears were stiff triangles of attention; his head rose with interest.

"You have a good enough natural seat," Mrs. Portree called. "Straighten your back, not rigid, just straight so you're not hunching forward. Don't drop your head forward like that; it throws your weight off balance. That's better. Hands low, just a few inches above his withers. There, that's good. Take up the slack in the reins. Pull them through your hands so you can feel his mouth at the far end of them. Just feel it lightly, don't restrict it. Remember, a horse needs to bob his head with every step, so give with your arms, move your arms forward in rhythm with him so you keep that contact without hitting him in the mouth with every step. There, that's better."

Addie was unaware of the grin on her own face. It was the unconscious reflection of her joy.

"Take him around the house. Don't pull on the

56

rein to turn him, just squeeze it lightly and twist
your body in the direction of the turn. Imagine the
bit in your own mouth and don't pull any harder
than you'd want to be pulled."

Around and around the house Addie and Ribbon went, walking and then at a slow jog.

"Don't stiffen your back and you won't bounce.
Flex at the waist. Move your pelvis, swing it from
your waist. No, don't force it, just relax and follow
his rhythm."

After a few rounds Mrs. Portree went back to
weeding the bed of chrysanthemums that lined the
side of the house, but since she didn't tell Addie to
stop, Addie and Ribbon rode on, figure-eighting
around buildings and trees. With Mrs. Portree's eyes
off of them, Addie relaxed and stroked Ribbon's neck
as they walked. Today he seemed less like a magical
companion and more like an ordinary pony, but
that didn't diminish her love for him, nor her hunger
for signs of affection from him.

Once when they stopped, Ribbon swung his
head around and smelled the toe of Addie's shoe,
butting it with his muzzle and taking it gently between his teeth. He looked up at her as though
gauging her reaction, and she was not afraid of his
teeth around her foot.

She understood what he was saying. "I am bigger and stronger than you, and I could bite you if I wanted to, but I choose not to. I choose to use my strength to carry you and serve you and take care of you, even though it is within my power to hurt you." Addie understood him.

After a while she rode him back to where Mrs. Portree was working, and let him graze while she lay atop his neck, breathing in the fragrance of him.

"I wonder why horses let us ride them," she mused aloud. "They wouldn't have to. They could fight us off and do whatever they wanted. But they let us."

Mrs. Portree grunted. "Horses simply take the course of least resistance, girl. It's easier to obey us than not to. Simple as that."

Addie cocked her head thoughtfully. "Don't you love horses?"

"I was raised with them. I grew up in Virginia, in the hunt country. Everyone there rode. We belonged to one of the finest hunt clubs this side of England. Children there belonged to Pony Clubs the way youngsters around here belong to Little League. We all learned to ride and jump at a very early age."

"Yes, but do you love horses?"

Mrs. Portree weeded silently.

"You must love Ribbon a lot," Addie insisted.

"He was Madeline's."

Addie rested her cheek against Ribbon's mane and absorbed this knowledge. Mrs. Portree didn't love Ribbon; she loved Madeline and that was enough to make her clean Ribbon's stall and carry food to him for twenty years.

Addie thought about her own mother and about Alice Everett. Her eyes followed Mrs. Portree's back as it moved against the weeds. Addie was full of ache.

She wondered, resentfully, whether Madeline appreciated her mother.

7

After that day Addie became a miser with her visits to Ribbon and Mrs. Portree. She lived in fear of becoming a nuisance by going there too often, so she made herself stay away every other day.

On alternate mornings she darted across the highway, circled the Allens' yard, pausing to greet Rosie and Duke and Idiot through their chain-link fence, hiked along the creek bank past the cornfield, then ducked through Ribbon's fence and ran across his grass, loving the field because it was his place, even loving the brown heaps of his manure.

Always she went to the house to announce her presence. Always Mrs. Portree was there. She was never gone visiting friends, or even shopping. As the number of visits mounted, Addie came to understand that her first instincts were right; Mrs. Portree was a solitary in Amherst, Wisconsin.

Addie's afternoons took on a pattern: lead Ribbon into the barn for a long luxurious grooming, using brushes and currycomb and hoof pick as Mrs. Portree had showed her; then on with the bridle, always handling his ears as though they were delicate birds in her hand.

After the first few days the rides were no longer lessons. Mrs. Portree trusted Addie to not run Ribbon nor to ride him on rocks, because of his unshod feet. Addie rode in the pasture or down the road, staying on the grassy edges, while Mrs. Portree watched from the yard or the windows of her house.

After the ride Ribbon got another brushing, just for fun, and an apple on Addie's flattened palm. Then Addie, or Addie and Mrs. Portree, dug the manure out of his bedding with the long-handled manure fork, and stirred the straw around, searching for wet places that must be removed. They scattered new straw in the thin spots and filled his water tank if it needed it, although he drank mostly from the creek.

Often, then, they stood side by side against the fence and talked while Ribbon dozed close to their

61

voices. It was always a wonder to Addie that between the two of them they ever found things to talk about. Mrs. Portree didn't much like talking about Madeline, or Mr. Portree, who apparently was not dead after all, but living in Ohio near Madeline.

Addie was leery of the subject of Madeline, too. Jealousy got in the way of whatever curiosity she had about her. And Mrs. Portree's life offered little in the way of conversational material; she took care of her house and yard and Ribbon, and that seemed to be all she did.

As for Addie, she told about her mother and Dutch, about Alice and Walt and Walt Junior and Lori and the expected baby, but she couldn't tell whether Mrs. Portree was interested or even listening. When school began Addie told Mrs. Portree about her teachers and doing gymnastics in Phys. Ed., but she didn't say much about her friends there. They didn't seem important even to Addie, much less to Mrs. Portree.

And often their visits were made up more of silences than conversation. They might stand for several minutes against Ribbon's fence, following him with their eyes as he moved around the paddock or stood slack-hipped, napping.

"I think he's slimming down a little," Addie would say, having said it before several times. After a long pause Mrs. Portree would say, "I think so."

Or the woman might say, "I believe I'd better dig up the bulbs tomorrow or the next day. It could freeze any time now." And Addie would nod and pretend she had a valid opinion about flower bulbs.

It was an odd, silent friendship, and yet it endured through those first weeks when it might have been killed by either of them, Addie not coming over or Mrs. Portree not wanting her to. The friendship, if it could be called that, was rough textured and knotty, and something of a surprise to both of them. But it did exist, and over the weeks of autumn it grew slowly, one strand at a time, one day, one shared smile at a time.

One night early in November Addie was awakened by Walt's hand shaking her shoulder. She was sleeping in Lori's room for the winter, and even in her fuzzy-mindedness she remembered to keep her voice low. Lori had had a bad sore throat all week and whined a lot and was more bearable company when she was asleep than awake.

"Is it time?" Addie asked him.

"Yeah, Alice has started labor. I'm taking her to the hospital now, Addie, so you're in charge here, honey. You can take the day off from school tomorrow to stay with Lori, okay? Alice's mother will be here by afternoon. I'll call you from the hospital as soon as the baby's born."

Addie nodded and went back to sleep.

The next morning she played mother, fixing breakfast for Walt Junior who didn't understand why Addie got to stay home from school instead of him when it was his baby brother or sister who was being born. She fixed hot chocolate for Lori, and Cream of Wheat that would slide easily down a sore throat. She cleaned up the kitchen and put clean sheets on her cot for Alice's mother to sleep on for the next few nights while Addie shifted to the davenport.

Wistfully Addie thought about the empty bedrooms in Mrs. Portree's house. She thought about the space and quiet of that house and the warmth that came between her and Mrs. Portree sometimes, unexpectedly.

Around lunchtime Big Walt called to say the baby was born, a little girl seven pounds, three ounces. He sounded happy and tired. Soon after that, Alice's mother drove up. She had been at the hospital and was now moving in with her suitcase and her bag of special groceries, to take over the children.

Every time Alice's mother came to their house Addie had the feeling that the woman was startled to see Addie still living there. She could feel the question in the air: "What? That Harvey child still here?" So as soon as she could, Addie left the house to walk uptown to the post office for the mail. Amherst was too small a town to have mail delivered to its homes, so each morning everyone in town came to fetch their own, and sometimes their neighbor's mail, too. Usually Alice kept that chore for herself because it was such a good time to visit with people.

It was a raw day, all gray and brown and damp-cold. No wonder Lori had a sore throat, Addie thought as she zipped her own jacket up higher under her neck and walked with her head down, fists jammed into her pockets. She hated the coming cold because it was going to make it harder to get out to Mrs. Portree's every afternoon, as she was doing now. A trip that was just a pleasant run in the summer would be miserable, painful, and sometimes impossible on a sub-zero winter afternoon when, in addition to the cold, the dark would come by four-thirty or five.

Addie didn't know what she would do without Mrs. Portree and Ribbon, now that she had them.

She began to trot awkwardly, swaying her shoulders rather than taking her hands out of her pockets. The post office was a haven of warmth when she pushed in through the double glass doors. There was a bank of private boxes along the wall dividing the front room from the back, but Addie didn't have the key to the Everetts' box with her so she leaned across the counter toward Jens.

As usual when he wasn't busy, Jens was reading at his desk behind the counter. He was an angular Norwegian, sandy haired and going soft and thick around the middle. All he ever seemed to read was war novels, and that puzzled Addie. Jens had been in the Viet Nam war and lost a hand in it by picking up something live that exploded. If it were her, she would never want to read or think about war again, but apparently Jens was different.

"Mail please," she called to him.

He looked up, lay his book face down, and got to his feet. "You playing hooky from school today, Addie?" He reached into the back of the Everetts' box, fished out their mail, and handed it to her.

"Alice had her baby this morning. A girl, seven

66

pounds and I forget how many ounces. I had to stay home and take care of Lori."

"Throat still bad, is it?"

Addie nodded. It occurred to her that Jens knew everyone around Amherst. "Jens, do you know Mrs. Portree?"

"Who, Rachel Portree? Sure. Well, not very well. She's on the rural route so I don't see her all that often. Why?"

"I was just curious about her. I've been going out there to ride her pony sometimes."

"That old pony of Madeline's? It's not still alive, is it? Lord, that was, what, twenty years ago anyway. Sure, twenty years, because Madeline was in school with me. Well, with my brother, she was a few years younger than me."

"What was she like? Madeline."

Jens pulled up the tall stool that he sat on for lengthy conversations. "Madeline Portree. I always kind of liked her, myself, even though lots of the kids didn't. She always dressed better than any-body else and talked better, and then her mother was always hauling her off to horse shows on week-ends. Every time she won anything on that pony her mother would get a picture of it in the local paper. Nobody could stand Madeline."

He stopped talking to remember, so Addie prodded him. "Was she stuck-up?"

"I don't think she really was, if you ask my opinion. You know how kids are, though. They stick a label on somebody like that, that she's stuck-up, and everybody just accepts it as fact. Me though, I think she hated all that stuff, all that fancy riding and the English clothes she had to wear for it. I remember one time some of the kids who had horses were going to go for a trail ride on a Sunday afternoon, just a bunch, you know, down through the park and along the river. Nobody invited Madeline, nobody thought to. But she showed up anyway, in old jeans and riding bareback. I was there, my buddy had an old pinto and I was on behind him, and I remember the look on Maddy's face when she rode up. It was like she'd just won some sort of war. Triumphant, you might say. What I guess happened was she just snuck out without old Rachel's permission, just to have fun with the rest of us for a change."

"So what happened?"

Jens shrugged. "We had fun. Just horsing around, you know, swimming the horses in the river and Indian wrestling and like that. No big deal."

"But what about Madeline?"

"She had fun, too." Jens grinned. "At first the kids were kind of shy with her, you know, not talking to her too much. But then when we were messing around in the river somebody dared one of the guys to slide off his horse's rump and grab its tail and see if the horse would pull him, swimming, you know. So the kid did it, and then Maddy did it, and then the kids treated her more like she was one of the group, you know."

"Then what happened after that? Did she change?"

Jens shrugged. "Not really. It was just that one day. She probably caught hell when she got home, and never dared to pull anything like that again."

Addie thought about it for a long time, thought about what must have been between Madeline and Mrs. Portree.

"That was just before Maddy ran away," Jens said, twisting down off his stool.

"Ran away?"

He nodded. "Took off. She was probably, what, fourteen or so. I think, in my own personal opinion, Madeline hated that mother of hers with a passion. Well, think about it. Her mother kept making her act like she was better than anybody around here, so naturally the poor kid didn't have any friends. I think it's perfectly understandable that she'd take off and go live with her father."

"Is that what she did?" Opinions were shifting in Addie's head.

Jens nodded, then he grinned. "Her father had had a bellyful long before that. He took off with this gal from Point and I'll tell you, this town loved every minute of it."

"Why?" Addie was shocked, feeling what Mrs. Portree must have felt.

"Well, come on, Addie. I mean, the woman never stopped looking down her nose at this town from the first minute she set foot in it. People can tell, don't think they can't. There wasn't a single person in this town who wasn't tickled spitless to see Rachel Portree get taken down a few pegs."

"But that's so mean."

He shrugged. "Long time ago, kiddo. Lots of water over the dam and under the bridge since then."

"Do people still hate her then?"

"Nah, I wouldn't say hate. They just used to laugh at her, that's all. Thought she got what she had coming. Nothing worth hating. By now she's just part of the community like everybody else. But you make your own place in a town, Addie. Rachel

Portree never did want to be part of Amherst, and she never really was. But people accept her for what she is. A snob," he added with a grin, "but still she's part of Amherst in her own way, like everybody else."

"I wonder why she stayed," Addie said as she gathered her mail.

"Too stubborn not to, I guess."

"What about Madeline then, when she comes back to visit? Are people nice to her?"

Jens was already back in his book. "Oh, she's never been back. She nor her father, neither one. Tell Alice congratulations and I want to see that baby girl."

"I'll tell her."

Addie walked slowly home, her head full of Mrs. Portree.

8

That Saturday an ice storm came. It was the first day Addie had been able to get over to see Mrs. Portree since the baby was born, and she trudged through solidifying rain and brittle grass, determined not to miss this day with Ribbon and Mrs. Portree.

The sky was dark, even in mid-day, with clouds of purple and soft blues, and dingy yellow undersides. Ribbon was not in the pasture to keep her company during the long walk across it. She missed his company but was glad he wasn't out in the wet. As she neared the barn she could see the pale shape of his head, watching from the stall door.

She went in to visit with him, but he didn't need anything from her and there was no question of riding in this weather. And she was cold and wet.

She gave him a final hug and ran for the house. The kitchen windows glowed an invitation to her soul.

Mrs. Portree didn't hear her knock, so she went on in and found her friend in the kitchen. "I knocked but you couldn't hear me," she said.

Mrs. Portree was standing over the stove watching a skillet. "Addie. I didn't know whether you'd try to come or not, in this weather."

Addie prickled to attention. She heard beneath the words the fact that Mrs. Portree had wanted her to come, had hoped she would. Without thinking, Addie crossed the kitchen and gave her a hug.

"Well. What's that in honor of?" Mrs. Portree's voice was as raspy as always.

"Nothing. I just felt like it." Addie hung her jacket where it wouldn't drip on anything good.

"Are you still trying to wheedle Ribbon away from me? Here, stand back so you don't get splattered. This oil is hot. I thought I'd make us some funnel cakes. It's a good day for it."

"You knew I was coming, didn't you?"

Their eyes met then, and a recognition of their bond flashed between them.

"You ever make funnel cakes, Addie?"

Addie shook her head and sat down to watch while Mrs. Portree filled a funnel with runny batter, then drizzled it into the hot fat in the skillet, making elaborate lacy patterns with it.

"And no, I'm not still trying to wheedle Ribbon away from you. I still want him, but I don't think you'll ever let me have him. Will you?" she added as a challenge.

"No," Mrs. Portree said calmly. With a spatula she turned the lacy golden brown rosettes of dough, let them sizzle for another few seconds on that side, then slid them out onto a paper towel. "Reach down in that corner cupboard there, Addie, get that blue canister. We'll put powdered sugar on some of these and cinnamon sugar on the rest."

With a plateful of feathery funnel cakes between them and mugs of spiced tea before them, Addie and Mrs. Portree sat at the kitchen table and smiled at each other. Outside, the wind drove sleet against the windows and made the pines creak, but the kitchen was bright and warm and fragrant with sugary smells; in the barn, Ribbon was warm and comfortable and didn't need them.

"Tell me about Madeline," Addie said finally. "Tell me about her really. Jens was telling me about the time she went riding with some kids from town when she wasn't supposed to."

Mrs. Portree wrapped her knuckly fingers around her mug for the warmth of it. "What else did Jens tell you?"

The house was very still.

"He told me Madeline ran away from home to live with her father. I thought you told me she left because she grew up and got married. You told me she came back for visits. Jens says she never has. I thought you told me you wouldn't sell Ribbon because Madeline loved him." Addie's voice rose to a note of accusation.

Mrs. Portree sat hunched, staring down into the steam of her tea.

"I told you everything about me," Addie accused.

"Yes. So you did. So you did, Addie." She raised her eyes then and looked at Addie and the girl flinched away from the pain she saw.

"I suppose we all have our little fictions. I suppose I was telling you the way I wished it was between Madeline and me. I was not a good mother." She spoke with barren dignity.

Addie wanted to say, "Yes you were," to make Mrs. Portree feel better, but she knew it probably wouldn't be true. She waited.

"I was not a good mother to my little girl. I was not a good wife. My life didn't turn out to be what I expected it to be. I never intended any of this."

Addie knew Mrs. Portree had lost sight of her small audience and was talking to herself.

"When I met John Portree he was quite simply the handsomest man I had ever seen. I met him at a dance at the naval base there near our home, in Virginia. He was with someone else and so was I, but we fell in love and that was that. He was a Chief Petty Officer, and I wanted that life. A woman doesn't just marry a man, you know. She marries his life, too, and John Portree's life was supposed to have been that of a naval officer, based in exciting places around the world. I'd have been with others like myself. That life would have been right for me."

Addie waited for her to go on, then prodded carefully. "What happened?"

"Nothing very dramatic. We were married, I became pregnant with Madeline, and John decided to resign his commission in the navy and bring us back here to his hometown. He'd had a wonderful boyhood here, and this was where he wanted his child to grow up." Old bitterness flavored the words.

"But you hated it here, huh?"

"It wasn't my world, that was all. I was a Virginian. I couldn't fit in. I tried my best to make Madeline into the kind of person I was."

"Why, because you were so lonesome?"

Mrs. Portree's eyes met Addie's and widened for an instant. "Yes. Probably. I never looked at it in that way, but probably that was it. But of course Maddy resented it. Everything I tried to do for her, buying her Ribbon and taking her to horse shows, she hated all of it."

"She hated *Ribbon?*"

"Oh, maybe not the pony himself really. Just all of it. I can see now," Mrs. Portree sighed, "that Maddy had every right to resent me. I've had many years to think about it, think about what I did wrong, to drive her away like that. But I couldn't see it then. I needed Maddy, and she ran away from me."

The woman's face remained dry but Addie felt her inner tears.

"I don't think you were such a bad mother," Addie said in a low ragged voice. It was the only offering she could make.

Mrs. Portree's face bent into its difficult smile. "That's kind of you to say, but I know better."

"No," Addie said more firmly, "you at least wanted to keep your little girl. Some mothers don't. You at least wanted yours."

In that taut moment, the light over the kitchen table flickered once, then went out. The refrigerator ceased its background hum, and the house went shadowy dark.

Mrs. Portree pulled in a long breath that released both of them from the emotion of their words. "There goes the electricity. An ice storm like this, probably the lines are down somewhere. It could be hours before they get it fixed. See if the phone is okay, Addie. Call home and tell them where you are, tell them you'll stay here till morning, or whenever it lets up outside. I'll get the fire going."

Addie made the call, then found Mrs. Portree in the living room lighting candles. With added logs the fireplace blazed, making the room beautiful. Mrs. Portree settled into the wingback leather chair near the fire, and Addie nestled in the afghan in one corner of the sofa near her. Outside the big windows, the world was totally dark now. The window glass sparkled with frozen rain.

Addie was excited by the storm, by the chance to stay overnight. It seemed a part of a fantasy she hadn't quite allowed herself to consider. She huddled in the afghan, not so much for warmth as for holding in her joy.

Taking a chance, she said, "I still don't see why

you wouldn't sell me Ribbon, though. Especially if Madeline didn't even like him. I don't think you really love him, yourself. I'm not still asking to buy him, I just can't understand."

"Oh," Mrs. Portree lifted her hand to stroke back a wisp of hair, and her hand stayed atop her head as though it were holding in the thoughts, "I don't really know myself, dear. Possibly for the same reason I've held onto this house and my life here. I suppose it was a way of holding onto Maddy . . . or making it up to her in some way. I just wanted to hold onto that pony. Or maybe . . ."

She paused for a long inward-looking moment. "Maybe it was my own childhood I was trying to hang on to, do you suppose? That was the one good, happy time of my life. I was popular then." She slanted a genuine smile at Addie. "I was very active in Pony Club, and the other children liked me. I fit in with them, you see. I won quite regularly at our little Pony Club shows, but even so, the others liked me. I had real friends. My life hasn't been so full of . . . warmth . . . since then. And there was Sugarloaf. She was my first pony. I outgrew her by the time I was ten or eleven, but we kept her in the family anyway. She was a little dapple gray too, like Ribbon, only smaller."

Mrs. Portree smiled to herself then, not at Addie, and closed her eyes to see her memories better. Addie didn't interrupt.

"I expect what I was trying to do with Maddy was to give her my own happy childhood."

"That's not so bad, then," Addie reminded her gently.

"What?"

"That's not being a bad mother."

"It wasn't being a very wise one."

Addie smiled and shrugged, and Mrs. Portree smiled back.

One log simmered in the fire, its juices bubbling out the end of it and making a hissing noise.

"We'll have to cook our supper in the fireplace," Mrs. Portree said. "The stove is electric."

But neither of them wanted to move.

"Tell me something, Addie. Tell me why it was that you wanted Ribbon so very much."

Addie hunched and shrugged again, and pulled her knees up closer to her chest. The room was warm and dark and full of exposed emotion, and she felt able to say anything. "The first time I saw him, you'll think I'm crazy or something, but the first time I saw him I was just lying there in the grass, sort of daydreaming that I had this, well, like a private angel, you know, somebody up above who cared about me. Not God, somebody more personal than that. Just for me. I was lying there thinking, now would be the perfect time for my angel to appear or to send me something special, like a fairy godmother or an Irish leprechaun or something, you know, like that. And I opened my eyes and there was Ribbon. It was just . . . I don't know. Special. I got on him and he carried me away and obeyed my commands even though he didn't have to, and it seemed like he really was my angel, or that my angel had sent him to me because I needed to be . . . loved. It sounds dumb, but I just had this feeling."

Mrs. Portree didn't answer right away. When she did, her voice was gentler than it had ever been for Addie. "Did you think if you owned him that then you would be loved forever? Was it like that?"

Addie sat still, then nodded her head against her updrawn knees. When she looked up, Mrs. Portree was smiling openly, showing fine, even teeth. She said, "Then I would say we were both saddling that unfortunate pony with a tremendous load of unrealistic expectations, wouldn't you?"

Addie nodded again, and grinned.

"I still won't sell him to you."

"I know."

Mrs. Portree quoted: " 'We cannot make bargains for blisses, nor catch them like fishes in nets; and sometimes the thing our life misses, helps more than the thing which it gets.' Alice Cary. Wise woman, Alice Cary."

9

On a Sunday in March Addie and her mother drove
out of Amherst and turned onto the country road
that circled around the bluff to make the formal
approach to Mrs. Portree's house. They were greeted
somewhat stiffly by Mrs. Portree at the front door
and shown into the living room just as though Addie
didn't already know the way perfectly well.

Gloria settled herself nervously on the sofa,
hardly daring to look around at the gleaming comfort of the old, stone farmhouse. "I expect Addie
and you have talked all this over already," she said,
her eyes darting away from Mrs. Portree's steady
gaze.

"Yes. We've discussed it thoroughly."

Addie and Mrs. Portree exchanged quick
glances, reassuring each other.

Gloria spoke quickly. "Addie's stepfather, that is, my husband, well, he's just not very much of a . . ."

"She knows all about that," Addie said.

"I kept hoping and hoping I'd bring him around," Gloria laughed nervously, "but you know how men are. Just as stubborn as a mule on Sunday, as they say. Well, it's a matter of room, too. The trailer has two bedrooms but Dutch has to have the one for his office. He does his paperwork at home, there, you know. It isn't that I don't want to have her . . ." She seemed to be pleading with Mrs. Portree for understanding.

"Yes. I'm aware of the situation."

Gloria rushed on. "Well, and then my friend Alice, Alice Everett, you know her. We were best friends in high school. She just loves Addie, and I know she hates to see her go, but that little house, with all those children. The baby's getting too big now to sleep in with Alice and Walt, and it's just plain a matter of room."

"I want Addie with me," Mrs. Portree said flatly.

Gloria didn't have an answer for that. It seemed to surprise her. "Of course I'll pay you for her expenses. I wouldn't expect you to foot the bills for her."

Addie hated this. She wanted to get the formal part over with so the good future could start.

Mrs. Portree sat up straighter. "I'm not taking Addie for the money, please be clear about that. I will accept it because I think you must assume some sort of responsibility for your daughter. But I want Addie here with me because she is wonderful company for me. I am very fond of her."

Gloria was still then. She looked from Mrs. Portree to Addie and back again, and suddenly Addie's heart squeezed as she saw the pain in her mother's eyes.

"Come upstairs, Mom. I'll show you where my room is going to be." Addie stood abruptly and ran upstairs to the room she and Mrs. Portree had chosen for Addie's use. It wasn't Madeline's room, it was a smaller room that had been used only for storage, but it had one brick wall, the back of the fireplace chimney, and it had sloping eaves and a window seat with a view out over Ribbon's barn and pasture. Addie loved the room.

Nothing had been done to it yet. Official sanction from Gloria had to come first. But they had made their plans and marked pages in the wallpaper book and selected furniture from other rooms. Easter vacation would be filled with fixing the room and moving in.

After Gloria had toured the house and been led to the barn to meet Ribbon, the three of them gathered awkwardly at Gloria's car.

"I'll walk on home, Mom. I want to stay here a while," Addie said.

Gloria nodded. She looked as though there was something more she wanted to say. Mrs. Portree moved slightly away from them to give them privacy.

"It's okay, Mom," Addie said, unsure of what she meant.

"I'm real happy for you, sugar. This is such a nice house, and I know it's what you've been wanting, to move over here. But hon, I don't know. She seems like such a . . . sourpuss of a woman. Now, no offense, I'm sure she's very nice, but she just doesn't seem, you know, jolly. Not very good company for you."

Addie smiled. "She's okay, really. I like her lots." She had started to say, "I love her," but sensed that hearing it would hurt her mother.

"Well, if you're sure this is what you want. It certainly does solve the problem."

Addie's smile turned crooked. "I know I always have been a problem for you, haven't I?"

"I just haven't been a very good mother."

"You did the best you could." Addie was surprised to find that she knew this.

Gloria sucked in a deep breath and opened her car door, then turned to wrap Addie in a hug. "I'll be out to see you regularly, and you come see me whenever you can, hear?"

Addie nodded. As the car pulled away she turned with tremendous relief to Mrs. Portree.

"We did it," she caroled.

And Mrs. Portree said, quietly, "Yes."

Ribbon lived for another four years, growing slower and stiffer every year. On a night in June he died in his sleep. "He was living on borrowed time," Mrs. Portree said, and although she and Addie cried together, they could hardly grieve for a life as long and pleasant as Ribbon's had been. Rather, their tears were for themselves, for old pains and loves, for the parts of their own lives that died with the white pony.

They had him buried in the pasture, near the place where Addie had first seen him. It had rained the night before, and clouds of yellow moths gathered over puddles in the pasture. The boulders were green with moss, and the earth smelled rich and damp.

Slowly, leisurely, Addie and Mrs. Portree walked from the pasture back toward the house. The neighbor's tractor, which had carried Ribbon's body, went roaring slowly down the road, leaving the afternoon silent. As they walked together, Addie and Mrs. Portree leaned into each other in the companionable way they had.

"He was a good old pony," Addie said.

"Yes, he was. And we owe him a lot." Her arm tightened around Addie's waist.

Through a cloud of moths they moved, stepping carefully around the wet places, miniature puddles gathered in Ribbon's hoofprints.

Addie said, "Do you remember a long time ago when I told you that I used to think my guardian angel had sent me Ribbon because I needed to be loved?"

"Um. I remember." Mrs. Portree smiled.

"I'm not so sure I was wrong about that," Addie said.

"Guardian angels do move in mysterious ways, their wonders to perform."

"Just what I was thinking."

They stopped to lean against the paddock fence and to smile at each other.